Three Stories
You Can Read
to Your Dog

Sara Swan Miller

Illustrated by True Kelley

Houghton Mifflin Company
Boston

For Marty, my husband
and fellow dog-watcher
—S.S.M.

To Jessamine and Jamaica
—T.K.

Text copyright © 1995 by Sara Swan Miller
Illustrations copyright © 1995 by True Kelley

Library of Congress Cataloging-in-Publication Data

Miller, Sara Swan.
    Three stories you can read to your dog / by Sara Swan Miller;
illustrated by True Kelley.
        p.   cm.
    Summary: Stories addressed to dogs and written from a dog's point
of view, featuring such topics as a burglar, bones, and running free.
    RNF ISBN 0-395-69938-X PAP ISBN 0-395-86135-7
    [1. Dogs—Fiction.]   I. Kelley, True, ill. II. Title.
PZ7.M63344Th 1995   93-38856
[E]—dc20   CIP
                        AC

Printed in China

LEO 30 29 28 27 26 25 24
4500657161

Contents

Introduction

Does your dog sleep a lot? Do you know why? Maybe your dog is bored. When you feel bored, you can read a book. But dogs can't read.

Here's a good way to make your dog happy. You can read these stories out loud. Your dog will like them. They are about the things that dogs understand best.

Don't forget to pet your dog while you read. Dogs like that almost as much as hearing stories.

Come here, good dog! Sit down. Listen up.
This story is just for you.

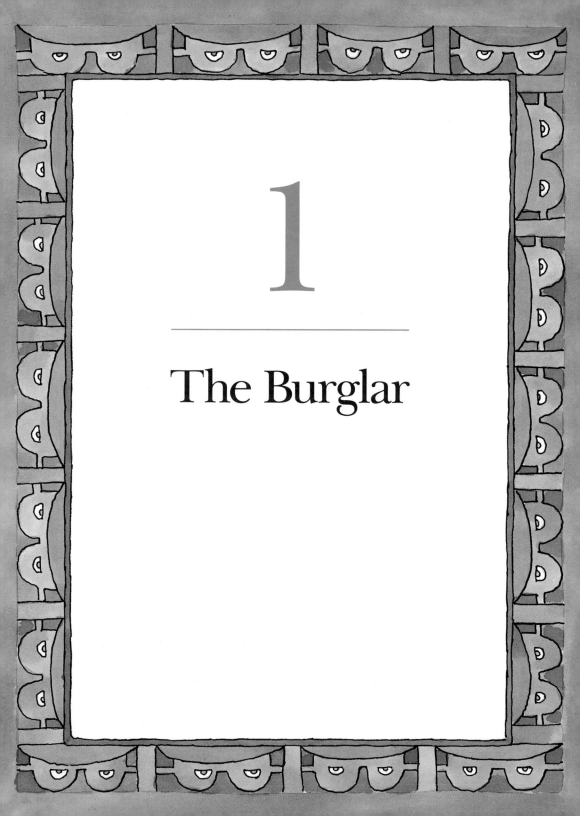

1

The Burglar

ONE DAY you were taking a nap.
There was nothing else to do.
All at once, you heard

THUMP! THUMP! THUMP! THUMP!

"Wow!" you said to yourself.
"A burglar! A burglar is knocking on the door!"

You ran to the door.

"Bark!" you said.
"BARK BARK ARK ARK ARK ARK ARK
ARK ARK ARK ARK ARK ARK ARK ARK
ARK ARK ARK ARK ARK ARK!"

Was the Burglar still there?
The door was big and thick.
You could not see what was on the other side.
Maybe the Burglar *was* still there!

"BARK BARK BARK!" you said.
"BARK BARK ARK ARK ARK ARK ARK
ARK ARK ARK ARK ARK ARK!"

Look! Your friend was coming to help!
Your friend was wearing big boots.
THUMP! THUMP! THUMP! THUMP!
went the boots.
"You silly dog!" said your friend.
"Stop barking! No one is there.
Look. I will show you."

Your friend opened the door.

The Burglar was gone!
You scared him away!

"What a big, scary dog I am!" you said to yourself.
"What a big, scary, brave dog!"

All of a sudden you felt very tired.
It is hard work being a brave dog.

You curled up on your bed.
And you went back to sleep.

Hey, good dog. Do you want another story?
Here is another one just for you.

2

The Bone

ONE DAY your friend went away.
You were left all alone.
Would your friend ever come back?
You waited and waited and waited and waited.
You waited forever.

Finally, your friend came home!

"Oh, wow!" you said. "Am I happy to see *you!*
I thought you would never come back!"

You wiggled and wiggled and wiggled all over.

"You silly dog," said your friend.
"I was not gone *that* long. I just went to the store.
Look! This is for you!"

Oh boy! A bone! A big, beautiful bone!
You grabbed the bone. You took it outside to your pen.

You chewed and chewed on the bone all day.
It was the best bone in the world!

"I need to put it in a safe place," you said to yourself.
"Then I can chew it again tomorrow."

You dug a hole. You put the bone in it.
Then you covered it up.

All at once you were tired.
It is hard work taking care of a bone.
You curled up and went to sleep.

You heard a funny noise in your sleep.
SHH SHH SHH SHH SHH.

You opened your eyes.

"Wow!" you said. "A bone tree!"

It was amazing! The bone had grown into a big tree!
It was covered with giant bones!

"Wow!" you said. "This is great!
Tomorrow I will have lots and lots of bones to chew!"

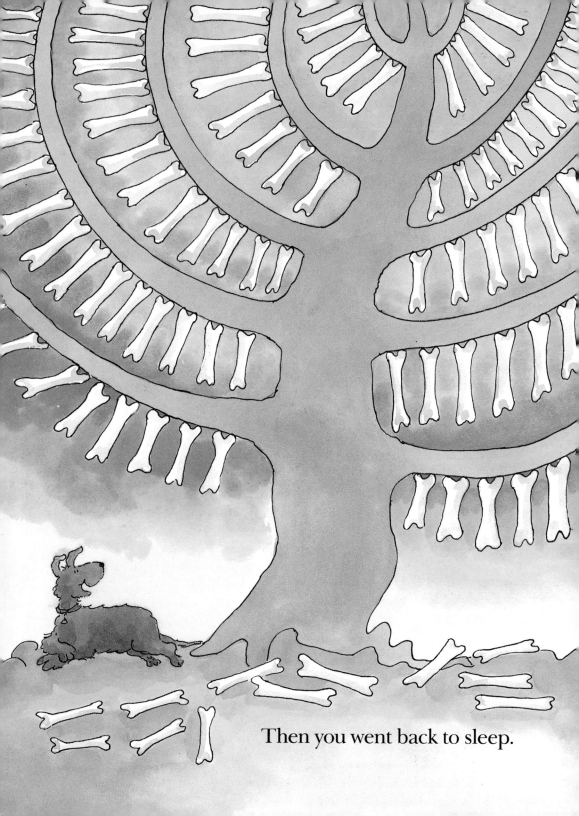

Then you went back to sleep.

A long time later, you woke up again.

Where was your bone tree?
IT WAS GONE!
Someone had stolen it!

You ran around and around.
SNIFF SNIFF SNIFF SNIFF!
But you could not find it anywhere.

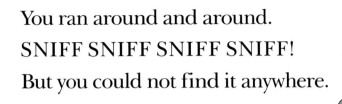

And where was your bone?
Maybe the bone tree *was* stolen.
But you could still have your bone!

You dug up your hole.

THE BONE WAS GONE, TOO!

Maybe that was the wrong hole!
You dug another hole.
And another.

You dug a hundred holes.
The bone was gone for good.

"This is terrible!" you said to yourself.

Then you had a good idea.
You would tell your friend to get another one.

You scratched and scratched at the door.
After a year, your friend let you in.

"Bone!" you said.
"Bone bone bone
bone bone!"

"What is wrong with you, silly dog?" said your friend.
"And where is your bone?"

Your friend did not understand.

"Here, good dog!" said your friend.
"How about a dog biscuit?"

"Oh, well," you said to yourself.
"A biscuit is better than nothing."

You ate up the biscuit. You felt nice and full.
You forgot all about the bone.

You curled up on your bed.
And you went back to sleep.

Do you want another story, you good dog?
All right. This is the last one.

3

The Wild Dog

ONE DAY you were feeling bored.

"I am tired of being in this house all day,"
you said to yourself.
"I am tired of being a house dog.
I need to be free! I want to be a Wild Dog!"

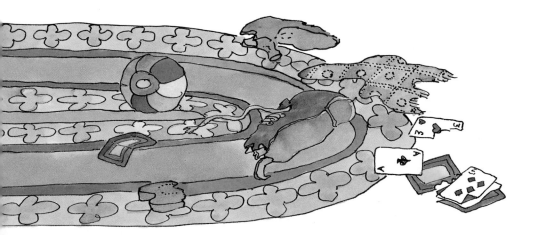

You went to the door. You put your nose in the crack.
Wow! It opened! You were free!

You ran out the door. You ran down the driveway.
You ran and ran down the road.

"Yay!" you said. "I'm a Wild Dog now!"

All at once a car came
running down the road.
It was running right at you!

"You can't scare me!" you yelled at the car.
"I'm a Wild Dog!"

You ran at the car.

"Bark BARK BARK!" you yelled at the car.
"BARK BARK ARK ARK ARK ARK ARK ARK!"

The car was scared. It ran right past you.
You chased it down the road.

"I am one scary dog!" you said to yourself.

"One scary WILD dog!"

You ran and ran and ran down the road.
Finally, you came to a forest.

"Just the right place for a Wild Dog like me!"
you said to yourself.

You ran into the forest.

Look! A hole in the ground!
You put your nose in the hole. It smelled great!
You sniffed and sniffed and sniffed.

Then you heard a funny sound.
Scuffle scuffle scuffle.
Oh, wow! A squirrel!

"Just the thing for a Wild Dog to eat!"
you said to yourself.

You ran at the squirrel.
But the squirrel cheated.
It ran up a tree.

"No fair!" you yelled.
"How am I going to eat you?
I can't climb trees!"

But the squirrel did not want to play fair.
It stayed in the tree.

"Who wants to eat a squirrel anyhow?" you said.
"I would rather sniff things."

You ran all over the forest.
You sniffed everything.
You sniffed a bush.
You sniffed a stump.
You sniffed a log.

You sniffed until your sniffer got tired.
All that sniffing made you hungry.

"What do Wild Dogs eat?"
you asked yourself.
You sat down to think.

"I know!" you said.
"I will find a nice can
of dog food!"

You ran all over the forest.

But you could not find a single can of dog food.

You sat down to think again.

"There are no dog food cans here," you told yourself.

"And what if I *did* find one? I could never open it!

I don't know how to work the opener!"

What a problem!

Maybe being a Wild Dog was not so great.

All of a sudden you knew just what to do.

You ran and ran and ran
all the way home.
You ran in the door.

"You bad dog, you!" said your friend.
"Where have you been?"

"Dog food!" you panted.
"Dog food, dog food, dog food. Please?"

"Are you hungry?" asked your friend.
"Do you want your dinner?"

"What a silly question!" you said to yourself.

The dog food was great!

"This is better than squirrels," you said to yourself.
"I think I will be a House Dog again."

You were all tired out.
Being a Wild Dog is the hardest work of all.

You curled up in your bed.
And you went to sleep for a long, long time.

The End